I LOVE YOU, BABY SHARK

Doo Doo Doo Doo Doo Doo

Art by John John Bajet

SCHOLASTIC

This edition published in the UK in 2020 by Scholastic Children's Books
Euston House, 24 Eversholt Street, London NW1 1DB
A division of Scholastic Ltd
www.scholastic.co.uk
London – New York – Toronto – Sydney – Auckland – Mexico City – New Delhi – Hong Kong

First published in 2019 by Cartwheel Books, an imprint of Scholastic Inc., U.S.A.
Copyright © Scholastic Inc., 2019
Adapted from the song, "Baby Shark".

ISBN 9781 40719 994 8
Printed in Italy

1 3 5 7 9 8 6 4 2

The publisher does not have any control over and does not assume any responsibility
for author or third-party websites or their content.

Papers used by Scholastic Children's Books are made
from wood grown in sustainable forests.

Wherever you swim,
be it near or far,
my heart will be with you
wherever you are.
From the light of day,
to the night so dark,
I will always love you,

BABY SHARK!

Hold you tight, doo doo doo doo doo doo.
Hold you tight, doo doo doo doo doo doo.

Hold you tight, doo doo doo doo doo doo. **HOLD YOU TIGHT!**

Day and night, doo doo doo doo doo doo.
Day and night, doo doo doo doo doo doo.

Give a hug, doo doo doo doo doo doo.
Give a hug, doo doo doo doo doo doo.

Give a hug, doo doo doo doo doo doo:
GIVE A HUG!

Safe and snug, doo doo doo doo doo doo.
Safe and snug, doo doo doo doo doo doo.
Safe and snug, doo doo doo doo doo doo.

SAFE AND SNUG!

Near or far, doo doo doo doo doo doo.

Near or far, doo doo doo doo doo doo. **NEAR OR FAR!**

Shining star, doo doo doo doo doo doo doo doo.

Shining star, doo doo doo doo doo doo doo.

Shining star, doo doo doo doo doo doo.
SHINING STAR!

Blow a kiss, doo doo doo doo doo doo.
Blow a kiss, doo doo doo doo doo doo.

Blow a kiss, doo doo doo doo doo doo.

BLOW A KISS!

Make a wish, doo doo doo doo doo doo.
Make a wish, doo doo doo doo doo doo doo.

Make a wish, doo doo doo doo doo doo.
MAKE A WISH!

Head to toe, doo doo doo doo doo doo.
Head to toe, doo doo doo doo doo doo.

Head to toe, doo doo doo doo doo doo doo.
HEAD TO TOE!

Love you so, doo doo doo doo doo doo.
Love you so, doo doo doo doo doo doo.
Love you so, doo doo doo doo doo doo.

I LOVE YOU, BABY SHARK DANCE!

HOLD YOU TIGHT!
Cross your arms in front tightly and rock back and forth.

DAY AND NIGHT!
Bring your hands together over your head to make a hand circle.

GIVE A HUG!
Bring your arms together for a hug.

SAFE AND SNUG!
Rock your arms like a cradle.

NEAR OR FAR!
Point here and there.

SHINING STAR!
Starting above your head, wiggle your fingers back and forth like star dust.

BLOW A KISS!
Blow a kiss.

MAKE A WISH!
Move your finger across the sky.

HEAD TO TOE!
Point from your head down to your toes and back.

LOVE YOU SO!
Make heart hands.